TWINKLE, TWINKLE

TWINKLE, TWINKLE

An Animal Lover's MOTHER GOOSE

Painted and photographed by

Bobbi Fabian

Dutton Children's Books　•　New York

CIP Data is available.

Published in the United States 1997 by Dutton Children's Books,

a division of Penguin Books USA Inc.

375 Hudson Street, New York, New York 10014

Originally published in Australia 1996

by William Heinemann Australia, Victoria,

a part of Reed Books Pty Ltd

Typography by Semadar Megged

Produced by Mandarin Offset

First American Edition

ISBN 0-525-45906-5

2 4 6 8 10 9 7 5 3 1

In memory of my little companion, and to those who know the enjoyment of animals

We would like to thank the following for their valuable contributions: Sandra Weaver-Hall, for her felines; Sally, from Command Dog Training School; Pat Morris, for her pigs; Myuna Community Farm, for the rabbits and lambs; and the Guide Dog Association of Victoria, for the six Labrador puppies.

CONTENTS

OLD MOTHER HUBBARD

Went to the cupboard,

To fetch her poor dog a bone.

But when she got there

The cupboard was bare,

And so the poor dog had none.

MARY HAD A LITTLE LAMB,

His fleece was white as snow.

And everywhere that Mary went

The lamb was sure to go.

He followed her to school one day,

Which was against the rule.

It made the children laugh and play

To see a lamb at school.

Round and Round and Round the Garden

Like a teddy bear;

One step, two step,

Tickle you under there!

TO MARKET, TO MARKET,

To buy a fat pig,
Home again, home again,
Jiggety-jig.

To market, to market,
To buy a fat hog,
Home again, home again,
Jiggety-jog.

PUSSY CAT,
PUSSY CAT,

Where have you been?

I've been to London
To visit the Queen.

Pussy cat, pussy cat,
What did you there?

I frightened a little mouse
Under her chair.

RUB-A-DUB-DUB,

Three men in a tub,
And who do you think they be?
The butcher, the baker,
The candlestick-maker;
Turn 'em out,
knaves all three!

Hey diddle, diddle,

THE CAT

AND THE

FIDDLE,

The cow jumped over the moon;

The little dog laughed

To see such fun,

And the dish ran away with the spoon.

THREE LITTLE KITTENS,

They lost their mittens,
And they began to cry,
Oh, Mother dear, we sadly fear
Our mittens we have lost.
What! lost your mittens,
You naughty kittens!
Then you shall have no pie.
Mee-ow, mee-ow, mee-ow.
No, you shall have no pie.

The three little kittens,
They found their mittens,
And they began to cry,
Oh, Mother dear,
See here, see here,
Our mittens we have found.
Put on your mittens,
You silly kittens,
And you shall have some pie.
Purr-r, purr-r, purr-r.
Oh, let us have some pie.

JACK BE NIMBLE,

Jack be quick,

Jack **jump** over

The **candlestick.**

THERE WAS AN OLD WOMAN who lived in a shoe.

She had so many children she didn't know what to do.

She gave them some broth without any bread,

Then whipped them all soundly and put them to bed.

BARBER, BARBER,

How many hairs will make a **wig?**

shave a **pig.**

Four and twenty, that's **enough.**

Give the barber a pinch of **snuff.**

ROCK-A-BYE, BABY,

on the tree top,

When the wind blows the cradle will rock.

When the bough breaks, the cradle will fall,

And down will come baby, cradle and all.

TWINKLE, TWINKLE,

little star,

How I wonder what you are!

Up above the world so high,

Like a diamond in the sky.

Twinkle, twinkle, little star,

How I wonder what you are!

GOOSEY, GOOSEY GANDER,

Goosey, goosey gander, Whither shall I wander? Upstairs and downstairs And in my lady's chamber. There I met an old man Who would not say his prayers. I took him by the left leg And threw him down the stairs.

DING, DONG, BELL

Pussy's in the well.

Who put her in?

Little Johnny Green.

Who pulled her out?

Little Tommy Stout.

What a naughty boy was that

To try to drown poor pussy cat,

Who never did him any harm,

And killed the mice in his father's barn.

LITTLE BO-PEEP

Little Bo-Peep has lost her sheep
And doesn't know where to find them;
Leave them alone, and they'll come home,
Bringing their tails behind them.

Little Bo-Peep fell fast asleep
And dreamt she heard them bleating;
But when she awoke, she found it a joke,
For they were still a-fleeting.

Then up she took her little crook,
Determined for to find them;
She found them indeed, but it made her heart bleed,
For they'd left their tails behind them.

It happened one day as Bo-Peep did stray
Into a meadow nearby—
There she espied their tails side by side,
All hung on a tree to dry.

She heaved a sigh and wiped her eye,
Raced over hill and dale;
And tried what she could, as a shepherdess should,
To tack to each sheep its tail.